SHAKESPEARE
MADE EASY

Romeo and Juliet

Tanya Grosz and Linda Wendler

3120 Pullman Street
Costa Mesa, CA 92626
Web site: www.sdlback.com

ISBN-13: 978-1-59905-137-6
ISBN-10: 1-59905-137-0
eBook: 978-1-60291-427-8

Printed in the United States of America
13 12 11 10   6 7 8 9 10

Contents

To the Teacher

As any teacher or student who has read Shakespeare knows, his plays are not easy. They are thought-provoking and complex texts that abound with romance, deceit, tragedy, comedy, revenge, and humanity shown at its very worst as well as its very best. In short, to read Shakespeare is to explore the depths and heights of humanity.

The *Shakespeare Made Easy* Activity Guides are designed by teachers for teachers to help students navigate this journey. Each guide is broken into six sections of four activities and one review. At the end of each guide is a final test, a variety of culminating activities, and an answer key. The activities are meant to aid textual comprehension, provide creative opportunities for the reader to make personal connections with the text, and help busy teachers gain quick access to classroom-tested and age-appropriate activities that make the teaching of Shakespeare an easier task.

Each regular activity, as well as each culminating activity, can be modified to be an individual or a group task, and the reviews and tests can be used as quick comprehension checks or formally scored assessments. The guides may be used in conjunction with the Barron's *Shakespeare Made Easy* texts or alone. Ultimately, the *Shakespeare Made Easy* Activity Guides are intended to assist teachers and students in gaining an increased understanding of and appreciation for the reading of Shakespeare.

Introduction to the Play

Background to *Romeo and Juliet*

The story of Romeo and Juliet was known throughout Europe and England before Shakespeare wrote his version for the stage in about 1597. The main source for the play was the poem by Arthur Brooke entitled *The Tragical History of Romeus and Juliet.* Brooke's version, printed about 30 years before Shakespeare wrote *Romeo and Juliet,* emphasizes that Romeus and Juliet are ill-fated lovers and shows the contrast between their love and the hate between their parents. The legend behind his poem came from other literature in France and Italy. These earlier versions may also have influenced Shakespeare. One Italian version of the story is from 1530 by Luigi Da Porto. In his version, the young lovers are called Romeo and Guilietta. As in Shakespeare's play, Da Porto's story is set in Verona, Italy, and the young lovers are children of feuding parents, the Montagues and Capulets.

Even earlier, a similar story came from the Italian writer Masuccia of Salerno. In this account, two lovers are married by a friar in secret. The boy, Mariotto, kills someone in a quarrel and is banished. His lover, Gianozza, takes a sleeping potion from the friar and is entombed in order to avoid marriage with someone her father wishes her to marry. After she takes the potion and is presumed dead, the friar frees her from the tomb so he can take her to her lover. Mariotto does not hear about the plan, however, because pirates capture the messenger sent from from the friar. Mariotto arrives at Gianozza's tomb, is recognized, and is killed. Gianozza joins a convent and dies of grief.

Shakespeare was not afraid of using familiar material in his plays. However, Shakespeare made some interesting adjustments to the plot to give his play more passion and drama. Shakespeare took the action that occurs in Brooke's poem over nine months and compresses it into a few days. For example, in Brooke's poem, many days pass between the ball and Romeo and Juliet's meeting in the garden, instead of everything occurring on the same night. In Brooke's version, Romeo and Juliet are married for about two months, and each night Romeo visits Juliet by climbing up a rope ladder to her room. In Shakespeare's version, Romeo and Juliet only have one night together as man and wife. This collapsing of time makes the events of the play more tragic and emotional.

Due to the strong love story and the memorable characters, *The Tragedy of Romeo and Juliet* quickly became one of Shakespeare's most popular works. Even today, *Romeo and Juliet* remains a favorite because of the passion and sadness of the love story and the beauty of the poetry in the play.

Synopsis of *Romeo and Juliet*

Prologue

This sonnet gives the plot and theme of the entire play: the story of the romance of two young lovers. Because of the death of these two "star-crossed lovers," the parents of the children end their bitter feud.

Act one, Scenes 1 and 2

Samson and Gregory, who are related to the Capulets, express their hatred of the Montague family. This hatred is a result of an ancient feud between the two families. Servants from the house of Montague walk by, and Samson and Gregory taunt them. They begin to fight with swords. Benvolio, a Montague, tries to stop the fight, but when Tybalt, a Capulet, enters the scene, the fighting grows worse. Prince Escalus of Verona arrives and orders all brawls to end under penalty of death.

Romeo's parents, the Montagues, are worried about Romeo's moody sadness. They ask Benvolio to try to find out what is bothering Romeo. He talks with Romeo and discovers that Romeo is swooning with love over Rosaline, but she does not return his affection. Benvolio persuades Romeo to go to a masked ball given by the Capulets in order to compare Rosaline with other lovely young women. There, Benvolio argues that Romeo will see that he does not need to pine for Rosaline when there are other beautiful young women that Romeo could love.

Meanwhile, Count Paris is at the Capulets' estate, asking for permission to marry Juliet. Capulet gives his consent only if Paris wins Juliet's love and if he can wait for two years because she is only thirteen.

Act one, Scene 3

Juliet's nurse and her mother speak to Juliet about Count Paris's wish to marry her. They feel that Paris would be a good match for Juliet, and Juliet responds by saying she will "look to like" Count Paris, but will not proceed with any relationship without her parents' consent.

Act one, Scene 4

Romeo and his friends proceed to the Capulets' ball. On the way, Mercutio gives a long and beautiful speech about the Fairy Queen Mab, who can influence the dreams of people. Just as they are entering the dance, Romeo feels fear about the future.

Act one, Scene 5

At the Capulets' masked ball, Romeo instantly falls in love with a young woman whose beauty teaches the "torches to burn bright." He speaks to her, and they kiss. The beautiful young woman is called away, and the Nurse tells Romeo that his new love is Juliet, daughter and only heir of the Capulets. Juliet also learns that the young man she has fallen in love with is a Montague and "the only son of your great enemy."

During the ball, Tybalt realizes that Romeo has crashed the party, but he is forbidden by Capulet to cause any trouble at the dance. However, Tybalt swears to pay back Romeo later.

Act two, Chorus

In this sonnet, the Chorus tells how Romeo's love for Rosaline has died, and Juliet is now Romeo's new love. Even though they are forbidden to meet, their love is stronger than any other claim on their lives.

Act two, Scene 1

Mercutio and Benvolio look for Romeo after the dance. Mercutio makes fun of Romeo's affection for Rosaline, little realizing that Romeo is now in love with Juliet.

Act two, Scene 2

Romeo is in the Capulets' garden under Juliet's window. He overhears her as she says to the night that she is in love with Romeo. He tells her that he is in the garden, and they exchange passionate words of love. Juliet asks Romeo if he is willing to commit to marriage, and he says he will. They part with great sadness but look forward to a secret marriage.

Act two, Scene 3

Romeo meets the Friar, who is collecting weeds and flowers for medicine. Romeo tells the Friar that he doesn't love Rosaline anymore but loves Juliet instead and wishes the Friar to marry

them. The Friar is unsure of Romeo's heart since he changed his mind so fast. He cautions, "Wisely and slow. They stumble that run fast." Still, the Friar likes the idea of making peace between the Montagues and Capulets, and he agrees to marry the pair.

Act two, Scene 4

Romeo meets up with Mercutio and Benvolio. Because of his new love for Juliet, Romeo is in a more social mood, and Mercutio notes, "Now art thou sociable. Now art thou Romeo." The Nurse arrives looking for Romeo and asks if he is serious about his relationship with Juliet. He says yes, and tells the Nurse to have Juliet tell her family she is going to confession, but instead she will be married to Romeo at Friar Lawrence's cell.

Act two, Scenes 5 and 6

Juliet waits impatiently for the Nurse to return with news about Romeo. Upon returning, the Nurse is tired and out of breath, but she enjoys delaying the good news to Juliet. She finally tells Juliet to go to Friar Lawrence's cell where Romeo waits to marry her. At Friar Lawrence's cell, Romeo and Juliet once again declare their love for one another, and the Friar leads them to the church to be married.

Act three, Scene 1

Romeo is in the streets of Verona after his wedding, and meets his friends Benvolio and Mercutio. His friends are in an argument with Tybalt over Romeo's presence at the Capulets' ball. Tybalt turns his attention to Romeo and seeks to start a fight, but Romeo realizes that Tybalt is Juliet's—and therefore now his own—relative, and so seeks no fight. However, Mercutio, who is Romeo's best friend and a relative of the Prince of Verona, is insulted by Tybalt's accusations and begins to fight with Tybalt. Romeo and Benvolio try to stop the fight, but Tybalt uses that opportunity to stab Mercutio and kill him. Romeo loses his temper at the death of his friend and kills Tybalt. Afraid, Romeo runs away. The citizens and the Prince arrive on the scene, and Benvolio tells the story of what occurred. The Prince banishes Romeo.

Act three, Scene 2

Juliet speaks words of love and desire to be reunited with Romeo. The Nurse enters and tells Juliet that Romeo has been banished for slaying Tybalt. Juliet's sorrow is deep for Tybalt but even more for banished Romeo. She sends the Nurse to Friar Lawrence's cell, where Romeo is hiding, with a ring and the request that Romeo come to her at night to say good-bye.

Act three, Scene 3

In the Friar's cell, Romeo is extremely upset about all his misfortunes. The Friar tries to cheer him up but is unsuccessful. The Nurse arrives and tells Romeo that Juliet wishes to say good-bye and gives him her ring. Romeo leaves for Juliet's room with a warning from Friar Lawrence to be back before daybreak.

Act three, Scene 4

Old Capulet decides to go ahead with Juliet's marriage to Paris, despite the death of Tybalt. He is sure that Juliet will go along with his wishes, totally unaware that she is already married to Romeo.

Act three, Scene 5

Romeo and Juliet regretfully say good-bye after their only night together. After Romeo departs, Juliet's mother comes in her room to tell her that she is to marry Count Paris. Juliet refuses. Her father and the Nurse arrive, and Old Capulet is very angry at Juliet's attitude. He demands that she marry Paris or be cast out of her house to "beg, starve, die in the streets." Everyone leaves Juliet except the Nurse, who advises Juliet to marry Paris since Romeo is banished anyway. When Juliet realizes no one cares about her situation, she vows to go to Friar Lawrence for a solution or else kill herself.

Act four, Scene 1

Juliet meets Paris in Friar Lawrence's cell, where she has gone to seek advice. The Friar tells her to pretend to agree to marriage with Count Paris but then to take a potion that will cause her to seem dead. She will be put in the family's tomb, where Romeo, who has been told of the situation, will come and free her and take her with him to Mantua. Juliet would rather die than marry Paris, and she agrees to the Friar's desperate plan.

Act four, Scenes 2 and 3

Juliet returns from Friar Lawrence and tells her parents that she agrees to marry Paris. They are very relieved, and Capulet plans to spend the entire night getting ready for the marriage feast. Alone in her room, Juliet imagines the horror of waking up in the Capulet's tomb or wonders if the potion will kill her. She finally drinks the entire potion and falls upon her bed.

Act four, Scenes 4 and 5

There is a bustle around the house in preparation for Juliet's wedding. The Nurse goes to wake up Juliet. She discovers that Juliet is "dead," and everyone grieves. The Friar comes to perform the wedding and acts as a comfort to the family, stating that Juliet is now in heaven and they should not be so sad. Then the musicians, who have been dismissed because there is no wedding, make puns and jokes.

Act five, Scene 2

Unaware of Friar Lawrence's plan, Balthazar arrives in Mantua and tells Romeo that Juliet is dead. Romeo, upset and angry at fate, buys poison with the intent to drink it in Juliet's tomb and join her in death. Meanwhile, Friar Lawrence learns that Romeo never received the letter he sent informing him that Juliet was sleeping in the family tomb awaiting Romeo's arrival. The Friar gets ready to break into Juliet's tomb to be there when she wakes up.

Act five, Scene 3

Romeo meets Paris at the Capulets' tomb. Paris has come to bring flowers and perfume to honor Juliet's memory. Paris challenges Romeo to fight, and Romeo refuses at first, wishing only to join Juliet. But when Paris calls Romeo a felon, Romeo fights with Paris, and Paris is killed. Romeo places Paris in the Capulet tomb and then finds Juliet. He is amazed that she looks so lifelike. He gives Juliet a final kiss and then drinks the poison.

Friar Lawrence enters the graveyard about 30 minutes after Romeo takes the poison. He enters the Capulet monument to find Romeo and Paris dead. Then, Juliet wakes up. The Friar tells her that Romeo and Paris are now dead and she should flee with him. Juliet refuses to leave Romeo, and the Friar leaves her. She kisses Romeo and stabs herself.

The watchman finds the scene of death at the Capulet monument, and soon everyone arrives in the churchyard: the Capulets, the Montagues, the Prince, and finally the Friar. The Friar tells the story of all that went wrong. The Prince blames the deaths of Romeo and Juliet on their parents' feud. He says, "All are punished." In the face of such a tremendous loss, Capulet and Montague make peace with each other.

Character List for *Romeo and Juliet*

Characters associated with the Capulets:

Capulet: Head of the family in Verona in a feud against the Montagues. He is rich and is the father of Juliet; sometimes referred to as "Old Capulet."

Lady Capulet: Wife to Old Capulet and mother to Juliet

Juliet: Thirteen-year-old daughter and only child of the Capulets. At the beginning of the play she is willing to let Count Paris be her suitor, but falls in love with Romeo and marries him in secret.

Nurse: Confidante and caretaker of Juliet

Tybalt: A nephew of the Capulets who is a trained fencer. He has a fiery temper.

Count Paris: A young nobleman who wants to marry Juliet

Peter: Servant to Juliet's nurse

Samson and Gregory: Servants of the house of the Capulets. They show their membership in the serving class by speaking in prose about bawdy subjects.

Three musicians: These musicians are hired to play at the wedding of Paris and Juliet, but that wedding does not occur.

Page: An attendant to Count Paris

Characters associated with the Montagues:

Montague: Head of the family in Verona in a feud against the Capulets. He is also rich and is the father of Romeo; sometimes referred to as "Old Montague."

Lady Montague: Wife to Old Montague and mother to Romeo

Romeo: Son of the Montagues. At the beginning of the play, he is suffering with love for Rosaline, but falls in love with Juliet Capulet and marries her.

Mercutio: A kinsman of the Prince and Romeo's best friend. He is very witty and sharp-tongued.

Benvolio: A peacemaker. He is Romeo's friend and cousin.

Abraham: Servant to the Montagues

Balthazar: Servant to Romeo

An apothecary: A seller of poisons and medicines

Characters associated with the entire play:

Prince Escalus: Prince of Verona. He wants peace between the Montagues and the Capulets.

Friar Lawrence: Franciscan monk who wants to help Romeo and Juliet. He is knowledgeable about medicines and herbs.

Friar John: A Franciscan associate of Friar Lawrence

Other extras: Citizens of Verona, Maskers at the Capulet ball, Guards, Watchmen, and various Attendants

Chorus: A character who is not in the play but provides comments on the play. The Chorus in this play gives an overview of the plot and theme in sonnet form.

Shakespeare and Stage Directions

The plays of Shakespeare are so well written that they seem to leap off the page and come to life. However, the plays themselves have very few stage directions. Perhaps this is because Shakespeare's plays were performed in large amphitheaters that were very simple.

This was a time before electric lights, so the plays needed to take place during the day to utilize the natural light. The average time for a performance was between noon and two in the afternoon. Theater historians report that there were typically no intermissions; plays ran from beginning to end without a break and took about two hours.

The set might be painted canvas to illustrate whether the play was occurring in a forest or a town, for example. Sometimes the background was accompanied by a sign that indicated the place as well. Props were few and large: a table, a chariot, gallows, a bed, or a throne.

However, the audience in Shakespeare's plays expected a spectacle for the price of admission. Therefore, there were many devices to produce a gasp from the audience. For example, a device in the loft of the theater could raise and lower actors so that they could play gods, ghosts, or other unusual characters. Additionally, a trapdoor in the stage offered a chance for a quick appearance or disappearance. The actors could suggest a beheading or hanging with various illusions on the stage. Sound effects suggesting thunder, horses, or war were common. Music was important, and drums and horns were often played.

Most important to the sense of spectacle were the costumes worn by the actors. These were elaborate, colorful, and very expensive. Therefore, they often purchased these outfits from servants who had inherited the clothes from their masters or from hangmen, who received the clothes of their victims as payment for their services.

Though Shakespeare's stage directions are sparse, definition of a few key terms will be helpful for the reader. The following is a brief glossary of stage directions commonly found in Shakespeare's plays.

Selected Glossary of Stage Directions in Shakespeare's Plays

Above: an indication that the actor speaking from above is on a higher balcony or other scaffold that is higher than the other actors

Alarum: a stage signal, which calls the soldiers to battle; usually trumpets, drums, and shouts

Aside: words spoken by the actor so the audience overhears but the other actors on the stage do not. An aside may also be spoken to one other actor so that the others on stage do not overhear.

Calls within: a voice offstage that calls to a character on the stage

Curtains: Curtains were fabrics draped around a bed that could be opened or closed for privacy.

Draw: Actors pull their swords from their sheathes.

Enter: a direction for a character to enter the stage. This can be from the audience's right (stage right) or the audience's left (stage left).

Enter Chorus: a direction for an actor to come to the center of the stage and offer some introductory comments, usually in blank verse or rhyming couplets. In *Romeo and Juliet*, the Chorus delivers a sonnet, a form of poetry associated with love.

Exeunt: All characters leave the stage, or those characters named leave the stage.

Exit: One character leaves the stage.

Flourish: A group of trumpets or other horn instruments play a brief melody.

Have at: Characters begin to fight, usually with swords.

Pageant: a show or spectacle of actors in unusual costumes, usually without words

Prologue: an introduction spoken by the Chorus that gives an overview to the audience and invites them into the play or scene

Retires: A character slips away.

Sennet: a series of notes sounded on brass instruments to announce the approach or departure of a procession

Singing: a signal for the actor to sing the following lines as a tune

Within: voices or sounds occurring off stage but heard by the audience

Introduction to Shakespeare

A Brief Biography of William Shakespeare

William Shakespeare was born in April 1564 to John and Mary Shakespeare in Stratford-upon-Avon, England. His birthday is celebrated on April 23. This is memorable because April 23 is also the day Shakespeare died in 1616.

Shakespeare was the eldest of nine children in his family, six of whom survived to adulthood.

William Shakespeare's father worked with leather and became a successful merchant early in his career. He held some relatively important government offices. However, when William was in his early teens, his father's financial position began to slide due to growing debt. After many years, John Shakespeare's fortunes and respect were restored, but records indicate that the years of debt and lawsuits were very stressful.

Historians assume that young Will went to school and took a rigorous course of study including Latin, history, and biblical study. In 1582, at the age of eighteen, he married Anne Hathaway, who was three months pregnant. Studies of Elizabethan family life indicate that Anne's situation was not unusual since it was accepted that the engagement period was as legally binding as the marriage. The couple had a daughter, Susanna, followed by twins, Hamnet and Judith. Not much is known about Shakespeare during the next seven years, but his name is listed as an actor in London by 1592. This was a difficult time for the theater because measures to prevent the spread of the plague regularly closed the theaters.

Between 1594 and 1595, Shakespeare joined the Chamberlain's Men as a playwright and an actor. The acting company featured actor Richard Burbage, and they were a favorite of Queen Elizabeth I. During this time, Shakespeare was writing such plays as *Romeo and Juliet* and *A Midsummer Night's Dream.* Even though Shakespeare was enjoying great success by the time he was 32, it was dampened by the death of his son, Hamnet, in 1596. Soon after, Shakespeare refocused on his home in Stratford where he bought an estate called New Place, with gardens, orchards, and barns in addition to the main home. He still maintained a home in London near the theater.

In 1599, Shakespeare wrote *Henry V, Julius Caesar,* and *As You Like It.* The Globe Playhouse was up and running, with Shakespeare a 10 percent owner. This means that he was able to earn 10 percent of any show's profits. This business position helped him solidify his wealth.

In 1603, Shakespeare's reputation earned his acting troop the sponsorship of James I, who requested one play performance per month. Their name changed to the King's Men. By this time, Shakespeare had written and performed in almost all of his comedies and histories. He was proclaimed the finest playwright in London.

But Shakespeare still had what is considered his finest writing to do. He began his writing of tragedies beginning with *Hamlet* in 1600. In the following five years, Shakespeare wrote *Macbeth*, *Othello*, and *King Lear*. Why Shakespeare turned to these darker, more serious themes is widely debated by scholars. But all agree that these plays established Shakespeare's premier place in English literature.

Toward the end of 1609 through 1610, Shakespeare began to write his problem romances. These works, *The Winter's Tale*, *Cymbeline*, and *The Tempest*, are rich with mature themes of forgiveness, grace, and redemption.

After 1611, at the age of 47, Shakespeare moved back to Stratford exclusively, settling into life at New Place and enjoying a renewed relationship with his daughters, especially Susanna. He prepared a will, which has become famous for the request to leave his wife their "second best bed." Many have debated whether this is a sentimental or cynical bequest. In the same year that his daughter Judith married, 1616, Shakespeare died at the age of 52. However, it was not until 1623 that all his plays were collected into one manuscript, now referred to as the *First Folio*. The fellow King's Men players who compiled the manuscript, Heming and Condell, entitled it *Mr. William Shakespeare's Comedies, Histories, and Tragedies*.

Shakespeare's England

The age of Shakespeare was a glorious time for England. William Shakespeare's life in England was defined by the reign of Queen Elizabeth I (1558–1603). During her leadership, England became an important naval and economic force in Europe and beyond.

England's rise to power came when its navy defeated the Spanish Armada in 1588, when Shakespeare was about 24 years old. Queen Elizabeth was skillful in navigating through the conflicts of religion. She maintained religious independence from Rome as the Church of England became firmly rooted during her reign. Additionally, she financed the establishment of colonies in America to grow the British Empire and expand its economic opportunities. At the end of her reign, England was the leader in trade, naval power, and culture.

Because of its role as the main economic, political, and cultural center of England, London became the hub of England's prosperity and fame. If anyone wanted to become famous as a poet or dramatic writer during Shakespeare's time, he would need to be in London. In fact, London was full of great writers besides Shakespeare, such as Marlowe, Sidney, and Jonson. Yet, even as London was full of parties, trade, and amusement, it was also full of poverty, crime, and disease. Crime was a large problem, and the main jail in London was called the Clink. Disease and poor sanitation were common. In fact, twice in Shakespeare's lifetime, London endured an outbreak of the plague, which killed thousands upon thousands of people.

Before Queen Elizabeth took the throne, London was a modestly sized city of about 60,000 people. By the time James I took the throne at her death, more than 200,000 people lived in London and its suburbs. People were attracted to London because it gave many opportunities for work and financial improvement. It was also a vibrant social scene for the upper class. In fact, one honor of being a noble was the opportunity to house Queen Elizabeth and her entire party if she was in your neighborhood. If she was a guest, it was expected that her noble hosts would cover all the expenses of housing her group. She made many "progresses" through England and London, establishing her relationships with the nobility. However, several nobles asked to be released from this honor because the expense of supporting her visit had often caused them bankruptcy.

Perhaps it was better to be a flourishing member of the English merchant middle class. Their numbers and influence were rising in England at the time of Shakespeare. This was a new and an exciting development in Western European history. One major factor in the rise of the middle class was the need for wool for clothing. The expansion of the wool trade led to the formation of entire cities throughout England, and sparked progress in many other areas of commerce and trade.

With the rise of the middle class came a concern for more comfortable housing. Rather than serving simply as shelter or defense against attack, housing developed architecturally and functionally. One major improvement was the use of windows to let in light. Also, houses were built with lofts and special places for eating and sleeping, rather than having one multifunctional room. However, doors between rooms were still very rare, so that privacy in Shakespeare's time did not really exist.

Meals in Shakespeare's England were an important part of the day. Breakfast was served before dawn and was usually bread and a beverage. Therefore, everyone was really hungry for the midday meal, which could last for up to three hours. If meat was available in the home, it was usually served at this time. A smaller supper was eaten at 6:00 or 7:00 P.M., with the more wealthy people able to eat earlier and the working class eating later. Cooking was dangerous and difficult since all meals were cooked over an open fire. Even bread was not baked in an oven but was cooked in special pans placed over the fire. A pot was almost always cooking on the fire, and the cook would put in whatever was available for supper. This is most likely where the term "potluck" came from.

Furniture was usually made of carved wood, as woodcarving was a developing craft in Shakespeare's day. One important part of an Elizabethan home was the table, or "board." One side was finished to a nice sheen, while the other side was rough. Meals were served on the rough side of the board, and then it was flipped for a more elegant look in the room. The table is where we get the terms "room and board" and having "the tables turned." Another important part of a middle or an upper class home was the bed. Rather than being made of prickly straw, mattresses were now stuffed with softer feathers. Surrounded by artistically carved four posts, these beds were considered so valuable that they were often a specifically named item in a will.

Clothing in Shakespeare's time was very expensive. Of course, servants and other lower class people wore simple garb, often a basic blue.

But if a person wanted to display his wealth, his clothing was elaborate and colorful, sewn with rich velvet, lace, and gold braid. An average worker might earn seven or eight English pounds in a year, and a very nice outfit for a nobleman might cost as much as 50 or 60 pounds. In other words, if seven or eight healthy workers pooled their money for the entire year, spending nothing else, they could buy only one respectable nobleman's outfit.

Entertainment was an important part of life in Shakespeare's England. Popular sports were bear-baiting, cockfighting, and an early form of bowling. Bear-baiting, in which a dog was set loose to fight with up to three chained bears in the center of an amphitheater, and cockfighting, in which roosters pecked each other to death, were popular then but would be absolutely unacceptable entertainment today Bowling, however, has maintained its popularity in our current culture.

In London, a main source of entertainment was the theater. Some theaters were very large and could hold more than two thousand people. Even poor people could attend the theater since entrance cost only one penny (equivalent to 60 cents today), and they could stand around the stage. For a bit more money, a person could sit in an actual seat during the performance. However, some thought that going to the theater could be dangerous to your body or your soul. The theaters were closed twice during the plagues to reduce the spread of the disease. The Puritans disapproved of the theater as an unwholesome leisure time activity. And the Puritans also disliked the theater because the theaters were located in an area of London surrounded by brothels and bars. Nevertheless, the theater became respectable enough by 1603 to be supported by James I—and he was the monarch who directed the King James Version of the Bible to be translated.

ACTIVITY 1

Current Events in Meter

The Prologue

Background   The prologue is a 14-line poem called a sonnet. Each line has 10 syllables. The rhyme scheme is as follows:

ABAB CDCD	(first eight lines)
EFEF	(next four lines)
GG	(last two lines)

Directions   Look at a current newspaper and find a story describing a conflict of some sort (country versus country, person versus law, person versus person, and so forth). After reading the article, write your own sonnet based on the newspaper account. Look at the prologue as you write, using it as your guide for rhythm and rhyme. See the example below for an idea of how to start. Write your sonnet in the space below.

Example: Two women, quite unlike in every way,
In a parking lot (where this all occurred),
Were arguing—it turned into a fray
For miles around, their screams and shouts were heard.

ACTIVITY 2
Three Civil Brawls

Act one, Scene 1

Background   In this scene, Prince Escalus scolds the citizens for fighting as a result of the feud between Capulet and Montague. According to the prince, this is the third time that the fighting has disrupted the peace of Verona.

Directions   Imagine that you are a law enforcement officer in Verona during this time. Write three brief police reports (two to four paragraphs each) detailing the three civil (citizens versus citizens) fights. Cover the one you read in this scene last, making sure to include Prince Escalus's declared punishment for even one more fight (reread the passage if you didn't catch it). You know exactly what occurred during this fight, but you will have to use your imagination and what you know about the two families so far in order to describe what occurred during the first two fights. Write your police reports below. You may need to use another sheet of paper.

ACTIVITY 3

Love Is in the Air

Act one

Background William Shakespeare has many characters talking about love in this act, perhaps to foreshadow how the characters will react to the events that are to come.

Directions After rereading the following lines that each character speaks, write a few sentences that tell what these lines show about how the character thinks of or regards love.

Romeo (Scene 1, lines 170–178, 180–189):

Benvolio (Scene 1, lines 220–222; Scene 2, lines 46–51):

Juliet (Scene 3, lines 67–99):

Mercutio (Scene 4, lines 17–18, 23–24, 27–32):

ACTIVITY 4

Gossip Columnist at the Ball

Act one, Scene 5

Background   The fact that a Montague slipped into a Capulet party would have been big news for a gossip columnist considering that both families were wealthy and well-known. Several important things happen in this scene that should interest the people of Verona.

Directions   Imagine that you are a gossip columnist for the *Verona Daily Times*, and you have sneaked into the Capulets' masquerade ball. When people have their identities hidden, they are more likely to be free in their actions and words. Write a rough draft of the story you will run in the next edition of your paper. Be sure to include details of people who attended, any fights that occurred, and, of course, what goes on between Romeo Montague and Juliet Capulet at this fateful party. Write your story below. Use an additional sheet of paper, if necessary.

ACTIVITY 5
Review

Directions   Answer the following. Write the letter of the correct answer in the space provided. For 4, 7, and 10, write true (T) or false (F) in the space provided.

____ 1. In Prince Escalus's speech, we are told that the Capulets and Montagues have had how many fights?

    a. two
    b. three
    c. four
    d. five

____ 2. The play takes place in what country?

    a. Great Britain
    b. France
    c. Italy
    d. Spain

____ 3. Who attempts to calm down the feuding servants and keep the peace?

    a. Mercutio
    b. Tybalt
    c. Romeo
    d. Benvolio

____ 4. True or false: Romeo has been acting melancholy lately because he loves Juliet, but she is a Capulet and therefore forbidden to him.

____ 5. What advice does Benvolio give to Romeo about his troubles with love?

    a. send his love flowers
    b. look at other girls
    c. talk to his [Romeo's] parents about it
    d. talk to his love's father to try and get his approval

____ 6. How old is Juliet?

    a. 12
    b. 13
    c. 14
    d. 16

____ 7. True or false: Juliet is completely against being paired with Paris.

____ 8. How does Romeo accidentally find out about the Capulet party?

    a. He reads the guest list for an illiterate servant.
    b. He finds an invitation on the street.
    c. He overhears Capulet speaking to a friend.
    d. none of the above

____ 9. Why is Tybalt so angry at the party?

    a. He wants to dance with Rosaline, but she doesn't want to dance with him.
    b. He hates parties, but he was forced to go.
    c. He finds out that Romeo is there but can't fight him.
    d. He thinks Juliet is too young to be set up with Paris.

____ 10. True or false: As Romeo and Juliet are "falling in love" at the ball, they already know that their relationship will be forbidden because of who their parents are.

ACTIVITY 6

The Balcony Rap

Act two, Scene 2

Background   The balcony scene from *Romeo and Juliet* contains some of the most famous lines in all of literature.

Directions   Choose a section from the balcony scene between 12 and 15 lines long and turn it into a modern-day rap expressing the same sentiments. Be sure to incorporate rhythm and rhyme. Feel free to use a combination of Shakespearean language and modern language. Write your rap in the space below.

Example: But soft what light is breakin' yon?
It is the east, Juliet's the sun
Get up now girl and kill that moon
Yo so sweet I'm like to swoon . . . .

ACTIVITY 7

Love Opinionnaire

Act two, Scene 2

Background In the span of a few hours, Romeo and Juliet have fallen in love and arranged to be married, despite the hatred that exists between their families.

Directions Consider your feelings about "love at first sight" and arranged marriages. Then answer the following questions thoroughly. Use another sheet of paper, if necessary. Be prepared to discuss your answers with the class.

1. Do you believe in love at first sight? Why or why not?

2. Is there a certain amount of time that people need to spend together in order to truly know if they love each other? Explain.

3. In the play, Juliet is not yet 14, and Romeo is approximately 16. Marriage at this age was not uncommon in Elizabethan England.

   a. Do you feel that 14- or 16-year-olds can fully experience romantic love? Why or why not?

   b. Do you think that any teenager can be emotionally and mentally ready for marriage? Why or why not?

4. Though the concept of arranged marriages is strange to us, it still occurs in some places in the world. Can you think of any advantages of arranged marriages?

5. On a much smaller scale than arranged marriages, would you ever consider letting your parent(s) choose a date for you? Why or why not?

ACTIVITY 8

Friar Lawrence

Act two, Scene 3

Background   Friar Lawrence is understandably skeptical when Romeo, fresh from a crush on Rosaline, pleads with the Friar to marry him to his enemy's daughter, Juliet Capulet. The Friar does think that the marriage could soften the hate between the two families, though, so he agrees to perform the ceremony.

Directions   Imagine that you are the Friar, grappling with whether or not to support this relationship. Both the Capulets and the Montagues are wealthy and influential families with the power to cause you grief for performing this secret wedding. In the space below, write a journal entry from the Friar's perspective, contemplating the positives and negatives of aiding the young couple. Detail what you know of Romeo and Juliet as you weigh this decision. Use another sheet of paper, if necessary.

ACTIVITY 9
Figures of Speech

Act two

Background   Shakespeare uses many figures of speech throughout the play, some of which have become justly famous for their beauty and passion.

Directions   After reviewing the definitions of the figures of speech, read some examples from Act two and (a) identify which figure of speech is used in the line(s) from *Romeo and Juliet*. Then (b), write the meaning of each figure of speech *in your own words*.

Figure of speech	Definition	Example
Simile	Comparison using *like* or *as*	Her eyes shone like the sun.
Metaphor	Comparison stated without *like* or *as*	His kindness was an unexpected present.
Personification	Giving human characteristics to nonhuman subjects	The giant wave angrily swallowed the small ship.

1. "But soft, what light through yonder window breaks? It is the east and Juliet is the sun!" (Romeo, Scene 2, lines 2–3)

   a.

   b.

2. "Arise fair sun and kill the envious moon who is already sick and pale with grief that thou her maid are far more fair than she." (Romeo, Scene 2, lines 3–6)

   a.

   b.

3. "O speak again bright angel, for thou art as glorious to this night, being o'er my head, as is a winged messenger of heaven . . . ." (Romeo, Scene 2, lines 26–28)

   a.

   b.

(continued)

ACTIVITY 9
Figures of Speech (continued)

4. "Although I joy in thee, I have no joy of this contract tonight: it is too rash, too unadvised, too sudden, too like the lightning, which doth cease to be ere one can say 'It lightens.'" (Juliet, Scene 2, lines 116–119)

   a.

   b.

5. "My bounty is as boundless as the sea . . . ." (Juliet, Scene 2, line 132)

   a.

   b.

6. "It is my soul that calls upon my name. How silver-sweet sound lovers' tongues by night, like softest music to attending ears." (Romeo, Scene 2, lines 163–165)

   a.

   b.

7. "I would have thee gone; and yet no farther than a wanton's bird, that lets it hop a little from her hand, like a poor prisoner in his twisted gyves . . . ." (Juliet, Scene 2, lines 175–178)

   a.

   b.

8. "The gray-eyed morn smiles on the frowning night, check'ring the eastern clouds with streaks of light . . . ." (Friar Lawrence, Scene 3, lines 1–3)

   a.

   b.

ACTIVITY 10
Review

Directions Test your knowledge of the play thus far by determining which character spoke the following lines. All letters will be used at least once. Write the letter of the correct character in the space provided.

a. Romeo
b. Juliet
c. Friar Lawrence

d. the Nurse
e. Benvolio
f. Prince Escalus

g. Mercutio
h. Tybalt
i. Lady Capulet

_____ 1. "If ever you disturb our streets again your lives shall pay the forfeit of the peace."

_____ 2. "I hate the word as I hate hell, all Montagues, and thee."

_____ 3. "So please you step aside; I'll know his grievance or be much denied."

_____ 4. "I'll look to like, if looking liking move, but no more deep will I endart mine eye than your consent gives strength to make it fly."

_____ 5. "O then I see Queen Mab hath been with you."

_____ 6. "Speak briefly, can you like of Paris's love?"

_____ 7. "Then hie you hence to Friar Lawrence's cell; there stays a husband to make you a wife."

_____ 8. "I should have been more strange, I must confess, but that thou overheard'st, ere I was ware, my true love passion."

_____ 9. "Young men's love then lies not truly in their hearts, but in their eyes!"

_____ 10. "Did my heart love till now? Forswear it, sight. For I ne'er saw true beauty till this night."

ACTIVITY 11
Mad Mercutio

Background   In the beginning of Act three, Scene 1, Benvolio is trying to persuade Mercutio to come inside and escape getting into a fight with the Capulets. Benvolio knows that his friend Mercutio is hot-tempered and would never run from a fight. Throughout the first three acts, Mercutio's lines demonstrate a fiery personality.

Directions   Reread the following lines of Mercutio and decide what they say about him as a person. In the column on the right, write a sentence or two describing what you think the chosen lines show about Mercutio and the kind of person he is.

Line(s)   **Your Response**

1. "If love be rough with you, be rough with love; prick love for pricking, and you beat love down."
   (To Romeo, Act one, Scene 4)

2. "The ape is dead, and I must conjure him. I conjure thee by Rosaline's bright eyes, by her fine foot, straight leg, and quivering thigh, and the demesnes that there adjacent lie, that in thy likeness thou appear to us." (To Benvolio about Romeo, Act two, Scene 1)

3. "Why, is not this a lamentable thing, grandsire, that we should be thus afflicted with these strange flies, these fashion-mongers, these pardon-moi's, who stand so much on the new form, that they cannot sit at ease on the old bench? O their bones, their bones!" (To Benvolio about Tybalt and people like him, Act two, Scene 4)

(continued)

ACTIVITY 11
Mad Mercutio (continued)

Line(s)	**Your Response**

4. "Good Peter, to hide her face, for her fan's the fairer face." (To Peter about the Nurse, Act two, Scene 4)

5. "And yet thou will tutor me from quarreling?" (To Mercutio, Act three, Scene 1)

6. "O calm, dishonourable, vile submission!" (To Romeo, Act three, Scene 1)

7. "Will you pluck your sword out of his pilcher by the ears? Make haste, lest mine be about your ears ere it be out." (To Tybalt, Act three, Scene 1)

8. "A plague o' both your houses! I am sped." (To Romeo and Tybalt, Act three, Scene 1)

ACTIVITY 12

"O, I am fortune's fool"

Act three, Scene 1

Background   This is a pivotal scene in the play: Romeo tries to escape a fight with Tybalt (secretly knowing that Tybalt is now his relative), only to end up avenging Mercutio's death by killing Tybalt himself. When, in line 132, Romeo proclaims "O, I am fortune's fool," he is reacting to the realization that his actions could have dire consequences for him and Juliet.

Directions   In the space below, write a poem from Romeo's perspective, relating the events up to this point in the play that are important to him and his future with Juliet, trying to incorporate some of the emotion he feels after killing his wife's cousin (Tybalt). The last line should be, "O, I am fortune's fool."

ACTIVITY 13

Telling It to the Prince

Act three, Scene 1

Background   After Romeo slays Tybalt, the Prince comes to find out what started the fight and who is to blame. Benvolio recounts what happened, but Lady Capulet accuses him of lying in order to help his friend Romeo. She demands Romeo's death.

Directions   Imagine that you are a friend of Tybalt's who saw the entire fight, from Tybalt speaking to Mercutio at the beginning of the act to his death at the hand of Romeo. In the space below, write a speech similar to Benvolio's but from this friend's point of view. Interpret events slightly so that it does not look like Tybalt is the only one to blame. Use Benvolio's speech to the Prince as a guide for length and format.

ACTIVITY 14
What the Servant Said

Act three, Scene 2

Background   In Act three, Scene 2, Juliet experiences a range of emotions: eager anticipation, fear, anger, sorrow, shame, and so forth. She begins the scene as a new wife waiting to consummate her marriage and ends it grief-stricken over the fact that her cousin is dead and her husband is banished.

Directions   Imagine that you are one of Juliet's handmaidens. You are just outside her door waiting for her to call on you, and you overhear everything from her beginning speech to when she gives the Nurse her ring to give to Romeo. You run back to tell the other servants what has happened and what Juliet and the Nurse said and felt. Write your retelling below.

ACTIVITY 15
Review

Directions   Read each statement. Then write true (T) or false (F) in the space provided.

_____   1. Mercutio tries to talk Benvolio into getting out of the sun and avoiding a fight.

_____   2. Tybalt purposely comes looking for Mercutio to fight him.

_____   3. Despite the fact that Mercutio picks a fight with Tybalt, Mercutio blames the Capulets and Montagues when he is mortally wounded.

_____   4. The Prince decrees that Romeo be killed for Tybalt's death.

_____   5. When the Nurse returns with news of Tybalt's death, Juliet first gets the impression that Romeo is dead.

_____   6. Juliet gets angry with the Nurse for shaming Romeo.

_____   7. Juliet threatens suicide after finding out that Romeo is banished.

_____   8. Juliet is angry with Romeo for killing Tybalt and writes a letter to Romeo telling him so.

_____   9. After Tybalt and Mercutio fight, Romeo thinks Mercutio isn't really hurt badly.

_____ 10. Mercutio calls Romeo "King of Cats."

_____ 11. At one point, Mercutio jokes about his own death.

_____ 12. Romeo and Juliet have already spent a night as man and wife before these two scenes occur.

ACTIVITY 16

Romeo, the Outlaw

Act three, Scene 3

Background   Romeo is banished from Verona on pain of death, meaning that if he is seen in Verona again, he will be killed.

Directions   Create a "Wanted" poster for Romeo, including a picture of Romeo (what you imagine him to look like), what he did to get banished, the reward for reporting him, and any other information you deem necessary about this "dangerous killer." For an extra challenge, try writing the poster in Shakespearean English. Create your poster in the space below or use poster board.

ACTIVITY 17

The Friar Speaks Up

Act three, Scene 3

Background Romeo is so distressed over his banishment that he is weeping on the floor, talking about how death would be better than his punishment. He even goes so far as to attempt to stab himself, which prompts the Friar to get angry and rebuke Romeo for acting so immaturely.

Directions Read the following lines from the conversation the Friar has with Romeo. Answer the questions below the quotations that tell what the Friar is saying to Romeo.

"Hold thy desperate hand! Art thou a man? thy form cries out thou art; Thy tears are womanish, thy wild acts denote the unreasonable fury of a beast. Unseemly woman in a seeming man, and ill-beseeming beast in seeming both, thou hast amazed me."

1. What is the Friar saying about the mental and emotional strength of women? How does he regard women?

"Thy dear love sworn but hollow perjury, killing that love which thou hast vowed to cherish."

2. What is the Friar saying about the commitment that Romeo made to Juliet?

(continued)

ACTIVITY 17

The Friar Speaks Up (continued)

"What, rouse thee, man! Thy Juliet is alive, for whose dear sake
thou wast but lately dead: there art thou happy. Tybalt would kill
thee, but thou slewest Tybalt: there art thou happy. The law that
threatened death becomes thy friend, and turns it to exile: there
art thou happy."

3. What is the Friar saying to Romeo here about feeling sorry for himself?

"Go get thee to thy love as was decreed, ascend her chamber, hence
and comfort her . . . pass to Mantua, where thou shalt live till we
can find a time to blaze your marriage, reconcile your friends . . .
and call thee back."

4. What does the Friar suggest that Romeo do now?

5. Do you think the Friar was too harsh with Romeo, not harsh enough, or
   just right? Explain.

6. Do you think the Friar was justified in marrying Romeo and Juliet, or has he
   interfered where he shouldn't have? Why or why not?

ACTIVITY 18
Writing a Soliloquy

Act three, Scene 5

Background   At the end of Act three, Juliet delivers a brief *soliloquy*—that is, a speech when she is alone onstage and speaks her inner thoughts aloud so the audience can understand what she is feeling. In her soliloquy, Juliet expresses anger with the Nurse for suggesting she should marry Paris and forget Romeo. Right before the soliloquy, Juliet pretends to go along with what the Nurse has to say and tells the Nurse that she is going to see the Friar to ask for forgiveness for being disobedient to her parents. In reality, she is going to see the Friar to appeal for help in getting out of marrying Paris.

Directions   On another sheet of paper, write a soliloquy from Juliet's perspective expressing her thoughts and feelings about the recent occurrences. You may want to include the following:

- Tybalt's death

- Romeo's banishment

- Marriage to Paris

- Parents disowning her if she doesn't marry Paris

- What she will do to herself if the Friar can't help

- Missing her husband

- What would make her happy right now

- The Nurse's lack of loyalty to her and to Romeo

You may write the soliloquy in normal prose, or try a poetic form, such as blank verse.

ACTIVITY 19

Headlining   Act three

Background   There are many important events that occur in Act three, from Romeo in the streets of Verona after the wedding to Romeo and Juliet's sad good-bye to each other after their only night together.

Directions   Create newspaper headlines that capture what you think are the most important events of each of the five scenes in Act three. Keep in mind that headlines are generally fragments (not complete sentences) that draw attention through their use of vivid action verbs and alliteration (same beginning letters, such as **B**roncos **B**eat the **B**ears).

Scene 1:

Scene 2:

Scene 3:

Scene 4:

Scene 5:

ACTIVITY 20
Review

Directions Write the letter of the correct answer to each question in the space provided.

_____ 1. What does the Friar compare Romeo to as he scolds him for crying and carrying on about his banishment?

    a. fool

    b. baby

    c. woman

    d. child

_____ 2. What is the token that Juliet sends with the Nurse to give to Romeo as a sign that she forgives him for killing Tybalt?

    a. rope ladder

    b. scarf

    c. letter

    d. ring

_____ 3. After the young lovers spend their first night together, the next morning Juliet tries to convince Romeo that which bird is singing?

    a. nightingale

    b. lark

    c. robin

    d. dove

_____ 4. According to her father, Juliet is to be married on what day?

    a. Monday

    b. Tuesday

    c. Wednesday

    d. Thursday

_____ 5. What does Juliet's father threaten to do to her if she does not marry Paris?

    a. disown her

    b. beat her

    c. force her to marry him anyway

    d. imprison her

(continued)

ACTIVITY 20
Review (continued)

Directions   Beside each character's name, write the letter of the correct description.

_____ 6. the Nurse

_____ 7. Mercutio

_____ 8. Tybalt

_____ 9. Benvolio

_____ 10. Romeo

_____ 11. Lord Capulet

_____ 12. Juliet

_____ 13. Paris

_____ 14. Sampson

_____ 15. the Friar

a. refuses to allow Tybalt to ruin his party by fighting

b. wants to marry Juliet; has the blessing of her parents

c. makes fun of the nurse and angers her

d. issues a challenge to Romeo, then seeks him out

e. acts as the young lovers' confidante

f. first speaks well of Romeo then tells Juliet to marry Paris

g. tells the Prince how Mercutio and Tybalt were slain

h. gets in a fight in the first act

i. purposely "loses" his friends so he can chase a girl

j. defies her parents

ACTIVITY 21

The Friar's Plan

Act four, Scene 1

Background   The Friar has devised a plan to help Juliet avoid marrying Paris, but it is a dangerous and complicated one.

Directions   Reread the Friar's speech to Juliet describing the plan. Then in your own words, write a summary of each step of the plan.

    1. Lines 90–91
      Summary:

    2. Lines 92–93
      Summary:

    3. Lines 95–107
      Summary:

    4. Lines 108–113
      Summary:

    5. Lines 114–119
      Summary:

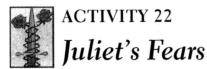

ACTIVITY 22

Juliet's Fears   Act four, Scene 3

Background   Before Juliet drinks the potion that the Friar gave her, she goes through several possible gruesome and frightening things that could go wrong with the plan in lines 15–58.

Directions   Choose one of her fears to illustrate as a poster to promote the play; you may draw in pencil or in color. Provide a catchy title for the poster and an explanation of the scene you have represented. Draw your poster below or on poster board.

ACTIVITY 23

Juliet's Letter of Explanation   Act four, Scene 5

Background In this scene, the Nurse goes to awaken Juliet only to find that she is "dead"; actually, she is just in a deep sleep from the Friar's potion. The Nurse, Paris, and Lord and Lady Capulet all go through mourning in this scene over Juliet's sudden and unexpected "death."

Directions Imagine that you are Juliet before she takes the potion. In the space below, write a letter to your parents that the Friar will deliver to them after you have woken and Romeo has taken you safely to Mantua. Explain to your parents about your marriage to Romeo and why you deceived them with your fake death. Plead for their forgiveness and acceptance of your new husband. Include anything else you think Juliet would need to say to her parents in order to receive their forgiveness.

ACTIVITY 24

Comic Relief

Act four, Scene 5

Background   Shakespeare often inserts humor in the midst of tragedy by using minor characters who are absorbed in their own world. At the end of this scene, despite the fact that the entire house is mourning the unexpected death of Juliet, the musicians and Peter still banter back and forth.

Directions   In the space below, create your own scene of at least 20 lines using these characters or minor characters (no more than four) that you make up. Try to make whatever the characters are discussing humorous, and attempt to use Shakespearean language. You may need to use another sheet of paper.

ACTIVITY 25
Review

Directions   Number the following events from the first four acts of *Romeo and Juliet* to match the order in which they occur, 1 being first and 10 being last. Write the correct number in the space provided.

_____   Prince Escalus banishes Romeo from Verona.

_____   Lord Capulet throws a masquerade ball.

_____   Romeo goes to Juliet's balcony.

_____   Romeo and Juliet are secretly married.

_____   Tybalt stabs Mercutio.

_____   Juliet drinks the potion that the Friar gave her.

_____   Juliet finds out from the Nurse that Romeo killed Tybalt.

_____   Tybalt and Benvolio fight after Benvolio tries to stop the servants from fighting.

_____   Romeo asks the Friar to perform the wedding ceremony.

_____   The Nurse finds Juliet "dead."

ACTIVITY 26

The Poor Apothecary   Act five, Scene 1

Background   When Balthazar tells Romeo that Juliet is "dead," Romeo is determined to take fate into his own hands; he decides to buy poison from a poor apothecary (pharmacist) so that he can end his life.

Directions   Imagine that the poor apothecary has a wife who has overhead his conversation with Romeo in lines 57–84. The apothecary's wife is scared, knowing that the apothecary could be put to death for selling the poison to Romeo. Create a dialogue (20–30 lines) between the husband and wife addressing her fears. You will need to use another sheet of paper to complete the project. You may use the following in your dialogue:

- what they will do with the money

- the apothecary assuring his wife he won't get caught

- speculation about why a rich young man like Romeo would need such a poison

- the wife's response (is she satisfied or still scared?)

ACTIVITY 27

The Letter

Act five, Scene 3

Background   The Friar recounts the events leading up to the young lovers' tragic deaths. The letter that Romeo never received telling of Juliet's fake death is handed to the Prince, and everything the Friar has said is confirmed by it.

Directions   In the space below, write the letter that the Friar intended for Romeo to read, but which now serves as an explanation of the tragic events. Be sure to include the following:

- the Friar's explanation of Juliet's "death"

- instructions about coming to the tomb to get Juliet

- plans for reconciling with everyone after going to Mantua

ACTIVITY 28
Obituaries

Background   In this play, Romeo, Juliet, Tybalt, Paris, and Mercutio all die.

Directions   In the space below, write the obituary of someone who has died in the play. Use your imagination to create details about the character's life that weren't expressly mentioned in the play, but be sure to use everything you do know about the character in the obituary. Read a newspaper to see what an obituary typically looks like (content, length, and so forth).

ACTIVITY 29

An Interview with the Friar

Act five

Background   Friar Lawrence is a Franciscan monk who tries to help Romeo and Juliet. He is an expert on medicines and herbs. Unfortunately, all his plans go wrong and both Romeo and Juliet die.

Directions   Imagine you are the most famous reporter from Shakespeare's time and you have been granted the one and only interview that Friar Lawrence will give before he vows to never speak of Romeo and Juliet again. Gossip abounds in Verona, and this will be everyone's chance to find out what really happened. In the space below, write your interview as a transcript, with your questions and his answers. Suggested length: $1\frac{1}{2}$–2 pages. You will need another sheet of paper to finish this interview.

ACTIVITY 30
Review

Directions Test your knowledge and understanding of the play by completing some of the lines from *Romeo and Juliet.* Write each answer in the space provided.

1. Juliet to her mother concerning marriage (Act one, Scene 3, lines 99–101):

    "I'll look to _____, if looking liking move, but no more deep will I endart mine eye than your consent gives strength to make it fly."

2. Romeo speaking to Mercutio before the Capulet ball (Act one, Scene 4, lines 106–108)

    "I fear too early, for my mind misgives some consequence yet hanging in the _____ shall bitterly begin his fearful date with this night's revels. . . ."

3. Romeo speaking to Juliet for the first time (Act one, Scene 5, lines 91–94)

    "If I profane with my unworthiest hand this holy shrine, the gentle sin is this, my lips, two blushing _____, ready stand to smooth that rough touch with a tender _____."

4. Juliet, upon discovering that Romeo is a Montague (Act one, Scene 5, line 135)

    "My only _____ sprung from my only _____!"

5. Romeo commenting on Mercutio's poking fun at him (Act two, Scene 2, line 1)

    "He jests at scars that never felt a _____."

(continued)

ACTIVITY 30

Review (continued)

6. Romeo commenting on Juliet's beauty during the balcony scene (Act two, Scene 2, lines 2 and 3)

   "But soft, what _____ through yonder window breaks? It is the _____, and Juliet is the _____."

7. Juliet during the balcony scene before she is aware that Romeo is there (Act two, Scene 2, lines 43–45)

   "What's in a name? That which we call a _____ by any other name would smell as _____; so Romeo would, were he not Romeo called, retain that dear perfection which he owes without that title."

8. Mercutio after being stabbed by Tybalt (Act three, Scene 1, line 87)

   "A _____ a'both your houses! I am sped."

9. Romeo after killing Tybalt (Act three, Scene 1, line 127)

   "O, I am fortune's _____."

10. Romeo after taking the potion (Act five, Scene 3, line 132)

    "Thus with a _____ I die."

Romeo and Juliet

Final Test

Directions: Read each statement. Then write true (T) or false (F) in the space provided.

____ 1. The play takes place in Rome, Italy.

____ 2. At the beginning of the play, Romeo is in "love" with Rosaline.

____ 3. Tybalt is Juliet's uncle.

____ 4. Romeo finds out about the party through an illiterate Capulet servant.

____ 5. Juliet is completely against marrying Paris when her mother brings up the subject.

____ 6. Benvolio is the one who tells Prince Escalus about what led to Romeo's death.

____ 7. When Romeo asks Friar Lawrence to perform the marriage, the Friar immediately says yes.

____ 8. No one realizes that Romeo is at the Capulets' ball.

____ 9. Benvolio delivers the "Queen Mab" speech.

____ 10. Juliet pretends to not know that Romeo is overhearing her during her first balcony speech.

Directions: Choose the letter of the best answer. Then write the letter in the space provided.

____ 11. What does "Romeo, Romeo, wherefore art thou Romeo?" mean?
   a. Where are you, Romeo?
   b. Why do you have to have the name of my enemy?
   c. Where have you been hiding lately, Romeo?
   d. none of the above

____ 12. What does Paris think Romeo is doing at the Capulet's tomb?
   a. defiling the bodies
   b. stealing treasure
   c. seeking forgiveness
   d. looking for a fight

____ 13. Which of the following is NOT one of the things Juliet fears will happen as she contemplates taking the potion?
   a. She will wake up before Romeo gets there.
   b. She will go insane and dash her brains out with Tybalt's arm.
   c. She will die because the potion is actually poison.
   d. Her parents will discover she is faking it.

(continued)

___ 14. What does Lord Capulet mean when he says to Juliet (after she has refused to marry Paris), "My fingers itch"?

    a. He wants to slap her.

    b. He is so upset about Juliet's disobedience that he is fidgety.

    c. He is referring to his wedding ring and inferring that Juliet needs one on her finger.

    d. none of the above

___ 15. Why does Romeo agree to go to the Capulets' ball?

    a. He will see Juliet there.

    b. He will see Rosaline there.

    c. He hopes to reconcile the two families.

    d. He wants to "crash" the Capulet's party and make them look bad.

___ 16. Why doesn't the letter telling Romeo of Juliet's fake death reach him?

    a. Friar Lawrence forgets to send it.

    b. Romeo's father intercepts it.

    c. The person delivering it gets quarantined because of the plague.

    d. It is lost during delivery.

___ 17. What do Lord Capulet and Lord Montague do in order to show respect for each other's child?

    a. They build gold statues of Romeo and Juliet.

    b. They agree to never fight again.

    c. They commission a building be built in honor of Romeo and Juliet.

    d. all of the above

___ 18. Who makes fun of the Nurse and angers her?

    a. Romeo

    b. Benvolio

    c. Tybalt

    d. Mercutio

___ 19. How does Juliet die?

    a. poison off of Romeo's lips

    b. self-inflicted stab wound

    c. a broken heart

    d. black plague

___ 20. Who speaks the last lines of the play?

    a. Lord Capulet

    b. Prince Escalus

    c. Lord Montague

    d. Friar Lawrence

CULMINATING ACTIVITY 1

Happy Ending?

Directions   The ending of Romeo and Juliet is so tragic, and the timing of Juliet awaking just *after* Romeo takes the poison makes it even more so. In the space below, rewrite the ending so that it ends happily; alter the events after Romeo is banished so that their lives do not end tragically. Suggested length: 2–3 pages. You will need to use additional sheets of paper to complete the ending.

Note: After you have written your ending, be prepared to discuss with classmates whether a tragic ending makes for better literature and why or why not.

CULMINATING ACTIVITY 2

Shakespeare's Words Today

Directions   Though far removed from our time and culture, Shakespeare's words and thoughts still fit many situations today. Find a line from *Romeo and Juliet* that fits a recent current event. Illustrate the current event (draw, paint, collage using clippings from magazines, and so forth) on poster board, adding the verse from the play that depicts it. Present your illustration and explain how your verse fits your chosen current event, or better yet, have your classmates see if they can guess the connection just by looking at your illustration and reading the line.

CULMINATING ACTIVITY 3

Retelling the Story from a Different Perspective

Directions   In small groups, retell the story of *Romeo and Juliet* from a different perspective. For instance, a well-known retelling of the story has actor Andy Griffith humorously retelling Romeo and Juliet's doomed love affair from a small town southern boy's perspective, using southern dialect to recount important dialogue. After discussing what perspective you want to use, type up a script for each member of the group and your teacher.

Guidelines

- No two groups may have the same perspective.

- Keep the retelling within a 5 to 7 minute time frame.

- As a group, decide which important events from the play you will keep.

- Attempt to stay in the dialect of your chosen perspective consistently.

- Don't alter the events of the play, just alter the language.

Some suggested ideas:
Gangster   Southern   Super Models   Political
Surfer   Reggae   Valley Girl   Hip-hop

CULMINATING ACTIVITY 4

The Verona Daily Times

Directions   Many of the events that occurred in *Romeo and Juliet* would have been news-worthy then as well as today. In small groups, work events from the play into a newspaper. Make sure to have the same sections that a real newspaper today would have (News, Features, Editorials, and so forth), using information and quotations from the play to supply and guide the content of your paper. Include "photos" of newsworthy events, quotations from characters, catchy headlines, and so forth. Use a real newspaper as your guide for format.

CULMINATING ACTIVITY 5

Romeo and Juliet, *the Condensed Version*

Directions   In a small group, choose only the most important lines and events from each of the five acts to compile a mini-version of the play. You may add a narrator to guide the action, but you must somehow fit the entire play into approximately 12 to 15 minutes. You must have a neatly typed script for every actor and one for your teacher. Your group must work out a way for the events in your mini-play to move smoothly. Use props whenever necessary, and practice so that you are more focused on acting than on reading your lines. Use the words of the actual text, adding your own words (in Shakespearean language so as to fit with the rest of your play) only when you are moving from event to event. When finished, you should have a brief (and probably humorous) rendition of the classic!

CULMINATING ACTIVITY 6
Who Is to Blame?

Directions   Write a multi-paragraph essay in which you prove who was to blame for Romeo and Juliet's deaths. A case could be made for many people: Friar Lawrence, the Capulets and Montagues, the Nurse, Romeo and Juliet themselves, and so forth. Be sure to support your assertion of guilt with quotations and events from the play. Consider going one step further—make a guess as to the outcome of the play if the character you blame had acted differently.

Activity 1

Answers will vary.

Activity 2

Answers will vary, but Prince Escalus decrees that the punishment for the next person who incites a fight on Verona's streets will be death.

Activity 3

Answers will vary, but the following is one possible interpretation:

Romeo: Love is painful, difficult, and emotionally consuming (Rosaline didn't return his affection).

Benvolio: Benvolio sees love as more of a crush; he thinks Romeo should be able to just look at someone else and forget his "love" for Rosaline (and he ends up being right about that!).

Juliet: Juliet's answer betrays how young and innocent she is. She has never really thought about being in love, but she is open to the possibility.

Mercutio: Mercutio takes a much more cynical (and sexual) view of nature; he finds Romeo's groaning for love silly. If Romeo wants a girl, he should just take her. His views are in line with his character; he lives for the moment.

Activity 4

Answers will vary, but they should incorporate the following events:

- Tybalt discovering Romeo at the ball
- Tybalt arguing with Lord Capulet, Capulet not allowing Tybalt to fight with Romeo, and Tybalt swearing to get revenge later
- Romeo and Juliet meeting and being enchanted with each other
- Romeo and Juliet finding out that the other is an enemy
- The fact that a Montague was at a Capulet ball

Activity 5

1. b	6. b
2. c	7. F
3. d	8. a
4. F	9. c
5. b	10. F

Activity 6

Answers will vary. For extra credit, students may put the rap to music and perform it.

Activity 7

Answers will vary because the questions require student opinions.

Activity 8

Answers will vary, but following is a brief example:

If either family discovers that I am the one who helped their secret love, I could be banished or imprisoned. I shouldn't have agreed to help Romeo. He seemed so sincere, though, and their alliance could soften the hatred between the families. If the families reconciled, things in Verona would be so much more peaceful. I must pray for further guidance. . . .

Activity 9

Answers to b. questions will vary slightly.

1. a. metaphor b. Juliet's beauty is so bright that it is like the sun shining through her window.

2. a. metaphor b. Juliet is so beautiful (like the sun) that she makes the moon jealous.

3. a. simile b. Please speak again (bright angel Juliet), for you are as beautiful and as glorious as an angel.

4. a. simile b. I am happy with you, but I am nervous about this; it is too fast and possibly short-lived, like lightning.

5. a. simile b. My generosity (and love for you) are huge, as vast as the sea.

6. a. simile b. When you (Juliet) call my name, it is like the softest music to my ear.

7. a. simile b. You should be gone (or you will be caught), but I would have you be no farther off than a pet bird, letting you hop only a little ways and then pulling you back like a prisoner on a thread.

8. a. personification b. The morning is gray and smiling on the night, flecking the sky with light.

Activity 10

1. f	6. i
2. h	7. d
3. e	8. b
4. b	9. c
5. g	10. a

Activity 11

Answers may vary but may include the following ideas:

1. This line shows Mercutio's cynicism about love and impatience with Romeo for being so melancholy about love.

2. This shows Mercutio's sarcastic wit and his tendency toward coarse and sexual talk.

3. Mercutio can't stand people who go with the ever-changing fashion and always try to be "in" or politically correct; he will always do his own thing.

4. This shows he will make fun of anyone, even an old nurse.

5. This shows he doesn't take criticism very well, and he will stand up for himself; he doesn't feel that Benvolio should talk to him about not fighting.

6. This quotation shows that he values courage highly; he thinks Romeo's kind words to Tybalt are embarrassing and weak.

7. This shows he is always ready to fight; he is egging Tybalt to do so.

8. This quotation demonstrates that he will blame others (like the Montagues and Capulets) for his own fault; he ends up dying because he picks a fight with Tybalt, but then blames the feuding families for it.

Activity 12

Answers will vary.

Activity 13

Answers will vary.

Activity 14

Answers will vary, but they should incorporate the following:

• Juliet is married to Romeo Montague.

• She is eager to spend the night with him.

- The Nurse came and was lamenting about Tybalt and Romeo; Juliet thought they were both dead for a moment.

- Romeo killed Tybalt, and Romeo is banished by the Prince!

- Juliet said something bad about Romeo, but when the Nurse echoed it, Juliet defended her husband.

- Juliet pleaded with the Nurse to give a ring to Romeo so that he knows she still loves him despite the fact that he killed her cousin.

Activity 15

1. F	7. T
2. F	8. F
3. T	9. T
4. F	10. F
5. T	11. T
6. T	12. F

Activity 16

Posters will vary.

Activity 17

Answers may vary but should include the following ideas:

1. He is saying that women are weak, and Romeo is acting weak by crying. The Friar is echoing a common view held back then.

2. Romeo is threatening to kill himself, so the Friar is questioning the seriousness of the vows he made to Juliet.

3. The Friar is showing Romeo all the ways in which he should count himself lucky—Juliet is fine, he killed Tybalt instead of the other way around, and he is banished

instead of killed. He should count himself lucky instead of whining.

4. Romeo should go to Juliet and comfort her. Then he should go to Mantua and wait until the Friar can work everything out so that he and Juliet can return to Verona.

5– 6. Answers will vary, as they are opinion-based.

Activity 18

Answers will vary.

Activity 19

Answers will vary, but use the following as a subject guide to each scene:

Scene 1: Tybalt slays Mercutio; Romeo slays Tybalt; Romeo is banished.

Scene 2: Juliet discovers that her new husband has killed her cousin.

Scene 3: Friar Lawrence concocts a plan to help Romeo and Juliet.

Scene 4: Lord Capulet arranges for Juliet to marry Paris.

Scene 5: The lovers spend their first night together; Romeo leaves for Mantua.

Activity 20

1. c	6. f	11. a
2. d	7. c	12. j
3. a	8. d	13. b
4. d	9. g	14. h
5. a	10. i	15. e

Activity 21

1. Tell your parents that you will marry Paris.

2. Go to bed alone (don't let the Nurse be in your bedchamber).

3. Drink this potion, which will make you seem dead for 42 hours.

4. When Paris comes in the morning, you'll be dead. They'll inter you in the Capulet's tomb.

5. I'll tell Romeo about everything, and when you awake, he will be be there with me and you will go to Mantua with him.

Activity 22

Posters will vary.

Activity 23

Letters will vary.

Activity 24

Scenes will vary.

Activity 25

Order of events: 7, 2, 3, 5, 6, 9, 8, 1, 4, 10

Activity 26

Dialogues will vary.

Activity 27

Letters will vary.

Activity 28

Obituaries will vary.

Activity 29

Interviews will vary, but the Friar's account to the Prince in Act five, Scene 3 may serve as a guide.

Activity 30

1. like

2. stars

3. pilgrims, kiss

4. love, hate

5. wound

6. light, east, sun

7. rose, sweet

8. plague

9. fool

10. kiss

Final Test

1.	F	11.	b
2.	T	12.	a
3.	F	13.	d
4.	T	14.	a
5.	F	15.	b
6.	F	16.	c
7.	F	17.	b
8.	F	18.	d
9.	F	19.	b
10.	F	20.	b

Culminating Activity 1

Endings will vary.

Culminating Activity 2

Illustrations will vary. You may want to assign quotations you think important.

Culminating Activity 3

Retellings will vary. You may want students to act out and tape their retellings outside of school. Some possible grading guidelines include:

• Smooth presentation style

• Dialect, events, and props appropriate for chosen era

- Typed script given to teacher
- Lines appropriately translated and para-phrased (didn't misinterpret play)
- Covered main events of the scene
- Complete script (including staging, setting, costuming, and dialect)
- Enthusiastic performance

Culminating Activity 4

Newspapers will vary.

Culminating Activity 5

Skits will vary, but you may want to consider the following when grading:

- Stayed within time limit
- Typed script given to teacher
- All group members had an active role

- Chose events of importance
- Showed enthusiasm when acting lines
- Used props where appropriate
- Clear to audience what was going on

Culminating Activity 6

Essays will vary. You may want to consider the following when grading:

- Used appropriate quotations
- Well-supported thesis
- Organized essay
- Didn't waffle with judgment of who was to blame
- Correct spelling and punctuation
- Demonstrated understanding of the play

SADDLEBACK
EDUCATIONAL PUBLISHING

MORE EXCITING TITLES

SADDLEBACK'S "IN CONTEXT" SERIES
(Six 112-page worktexts in each series)
- English
- Vocabulary
- Reading
- Practical Math

SADDLEBACK'S "SKILLS AND STRATEGIES" SERIES
(Six 144-page reproducible workbooks in each series)
- Building Vocabulary
- Language Arts
- Math Computation
- Reading Comprehension

READING COMPREHENSION SKILL BOOSTERS
- Read-Reflect-Respond, Books A, B, C, & D

WRITING 4
(Four 64-page worktexts)
- Descriptive Writing
- Expository Writing
- Narrative Writing
- Persuasive Writing

CURRICULUM BINDERS
(100+ activities in each binder)

ENGLISH, READING, WRITING . . .
- Beginning Writing 1 & 2
- Writing 1 & 2
- Good Grammar
- Language Arts 1 & 2
- Reading for Information 1 & 2
- Reading Comprehension 1 & 2
- Spelling Steps 1, 2, 3, & 4
- Survival Vocabulary 1 & 2

MATHEMATICS . . .
- Pre-Algebra
- Algebra 1 & 2
- Geometry

SCIENCE . . .
- Earth, Life, & Physical

STUDY SKILLS & TEST PREP . . .
- Standardized Test Prep 1 & 2
- Study Skills 1 & 2

SADDLEBACK'S HIGH-INTEREST READING SERIES
- Astonishing Headlines
- Barclay Family Adventures
- Carter High
- Disasters
- Illustrated Classics Series
- Life of...Series
- PageTurners
- Quickreads
- Strange But True Stories
- Saddleback's Classics
- Walker High

Visit us at www.sdlback.com for even more Saddleback titles.